Sarah's Questions

Harriet Ziefert

Sarah's
Questions

ILLUSTRATED BY
Susan Bonners

LOTHROP, LEE & SHEPARD BOOKS   NEW YORK

Printed in Japan.
First Edition

1 2 3 4 5 6 7 8 9 10

Library of Congress Cataloging in Publication Data
Ziefert, Harriet.   Sarah's questions.
Summary: A little girl asks many questions about the world while taking a walk with her mother. [1. Nature—Fiction. 2. Questions and answers—Fiction. 3. Mothers and daughters—Fiction] I. Bonners, Susan, ill.   II. Title.
PZ7.Z487Sar 1986   [E]   85-10947
ISBN 0-688-05614-8
ISBN 0-688-05615-6 (lib. bdg.)

For A.M.B.,
who poses inescapable questions
with consummate skill

Sarah and her mother had been working in the garden for a long time.

"Mama," Sarah said. "I'm tired of digging. Will you play 'I Spy' with me now?"

Sarah's mother answered, "As soon as I finish planting these seeds, we can take a walk. And we can play 'I Spy' along the way."

Sarah and her mother walked down the hill.
Sarah shouted, "I spy a fat, white cloud."
"I spy a little bird," said Sarah's mother.

904160

At the pond the jonquils and hyacinths were blooming.

Sarah said, "I see big yellow flowers—and purple ones too. And I spy a bee. And four baby ducks."

Quack, quack, quackity-quack! Where is mother duck?

Sarah stopped at Mr. Young's mailbox. She did
not say hello to Peter and Pumpkin. They were
both fast asleep in the sun.

Sarah's mother said, "Let's stop here and be very still and quiet."

Sarah tried not to move. She watched and waited. Then she whispered, "I spy a rabbit."

Sarah and her mother rested for a while on a grassy hill. Then they decided to walk home exactly the way they had come.

On the way home Sarah had a lot of questions.

"Mama," she asked, "why do squirrels have bushy tails?"

Her mother answered, "Animals have different tails because they need them for different jobs. Some tails are long and some are short. A squirrel's long, fluffy tail helps it keep its balance."

"I understand," Sarah said.

Peter was still asleep on Mr. Young's porch. Sarah asked, "Mama, do dogs dream?"

"I don't think anyone is certain about the answer to that question. What do you think?"

Sarah answered, "I think Peter dreams just like I do."

Sarah stroked behind Pumpkin's ear and under his chin. "Why do cats purr?" she asked.

Sarah's mother answered, "Cats purr when they are cozy and comfortable. Pumpkin is telling you he likes the way your hand feels."

When they reached the pond, Sarah asked, "Mama, why do bees buzz?"

Her mother answered, "Bees buzz because their wings move the air very fast. And the moving air makes a buzzing noise."

"Mama, how does a baby duck know who its mother is?"

"When a baby duck hatches, what it sees first is the dark shape of its mother. From then on, the duck recognizes that shape and follows it. If the duckling happened to see your shape first, it would think you were its mother and it would follow you!"

Sarah laughed at the thought of a duck being silly enough to think she was its mother.

Sarah heard the sweet sound of a bird.
"Mama, why do birds sing?"

"That is how they talk to other birds. Bird
calls can be loud or soft, shrill or sweet. When
the sound is pretty, we say the birds are singing."

Sarah and her mother were almost home,
but Sarah still had lots of questions.
   "Why are the clouds white?"
   "Why is the sky blue?"
   "Why does the sun shine?"

"Why does the hammock swing?"
"Why does the wind blow?"
Sarah's mother smiled and gave her a hug.
She said, "Right now you have more questions
than I have answers. Let's put on our shoes and
find Grandpa to see what he knows."

And that is just what they did.